The Lost Locket

Carol Matas

Cover art by
Tony Meers

Illustrations by
Susan Gardos

Scholastic Canada Ltd.

Toronto New York London Auckland Sydney
Mexico City New Delhi Hong Kong

Scholastic Canada Ltd.
175 Hillmount Road, Markham, Ontario L6C 1Z7, Canada

Scholastic Inc.
555 Broadway, New York, NY 10012, USA

Scholastic Australia Pty Limited
PO Box 579, Gosford, NSW 2250, Australia

Scholastic New Zealand Limited
Private Bag 94407, Greenmount, Auckland, New Zealand

Scholastic Ltd.
Villiers House, Clarendon Avenue, Leamington Spa,
Warwickshire CV32 5PR, UK

National Library of Canada Cataloguing in Publication Data

Matas, Carol, 1949-
The lost locket

ISBN 0-439-98973-6

I. Title.
PS8576.A7994L6 2002 jC813'.54 C2001-902738-9
PZ7.M42394Lo 2002

6 5 4 3 2 1 Printed in Canada 02 03 04 05

For my cousin Manny, best friend
and for Anna and Sylvia

The author would like to thank editor Diane Kerner for her support. Also thanks to Donna Babcock for the typing of the manuscript. And finally, to Dov Blank who loved the story and never stopped asking, "When will it be published?"

Contents

Chapter 1

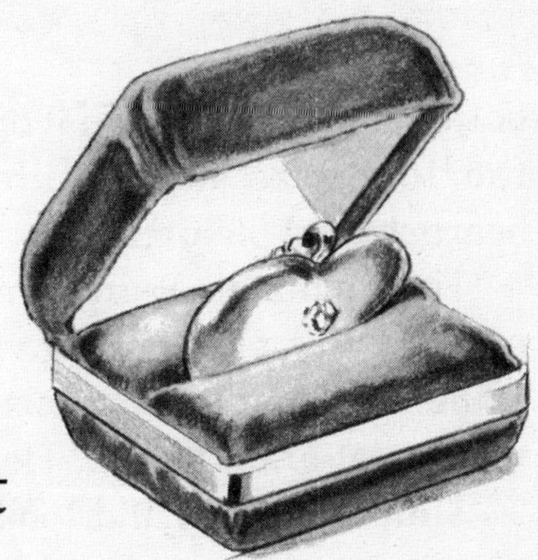

The Locket

It all started when Mother placed the small, square, blue velvet jewellery box on the kitchen table. She motioned me to sit down beside her. Then she picked up the box and opened it slowly. She gave me a meaningful look.

I realized that there had to be something awfully important in the box. Mom had even waited till Ben was in bed so we could be alone.

Slowly she lifted out a thin gold chain. Dangling on the bottom of the chain was a locket. It was shaped like a heart, with a tiny diamond in its centre. She pushed against the bottom of the locket and it opened. She handed the locket to me. Inside were two tiny heart-shaped pictures.

"That's your great-grandmother," Mom said, pointing to a nice-looking woman with a little smile and long curly brown hair, "and that's your great-grandfather." He looked stern.

I shut the locket and looked at it. The gold gleamed and the diamond sparkled.

"You don't remember your great-grandmother because she died before you were born," Mom said. "But today is her birthday. Baba gave me this locket on this date when I was eight, just the same age as you are now.

"Do you think you're old enough to take good care of this, Rosaline?" Mother asked.

She'd said my whole entire name. This had to be a very important moment.

"Yes!" I answered.

"All right," said Mom, "it's yours." She paused. "Don't lose it. And if I were you I wouldn't take it to school. It'll get lost there for sure."

I put the locket on the shelf above my bed, thinking it would look perfect with my white and pink dress.

I got ready for bed. I laid out my clothes for the next day at school. 'Course the locket would also look perfect with my green sweater, I thought. I was going to wear that and my black pants the next day. But Mother did say not to wear it to school. . . .

"Roz, didn't I tell you not to wear that to school?"

It was breakfast the next day, and I was wearing the locket with my green and black outfit. It looked great.

"Mom," I said, trying not to get mad, "I'm not a baby. I won't lose it. Honestly. I just want to show it to everyone."

She sighed.

I started thinking about all the games I could use the locket for at school. Like pretending it had magical powers. Or that there was a secret map inside it. Or — like in the book I'd been reading the night before — you spin it and suddenly you're in another dimension.

"Don't worry, Mom," I said, trying to sound very grown up. "You must trust me."

She sighed again. She shook her head.

"Let me see, let me see," squeaked my baby brother, Ben.

He made a grab for the locket. He's four. Right at that moment his fingers were covered in peanut butter. Come to think of it, they usually are.

"Ben!" I yelled. "Don't ever touch this." I threw on my jacket, grabbed my lunch and kissed my mother. "See you after school," I said.

"Don't forget I'm picking you up!" she shouted after me as I ran out the door. "We have some shopping to do."

"Okay," I yelled back.

Thank goodness I don't have to walk Ben to school. He goes in the afternoon so Mom takes him there and picks him up too.

After the bell rang and we had all hung up our jackets, Sam was the first one to notice the locket. (Sam is short for Samantha, and she's my best friend.) She sort of ogled my locket. Ogle is a word I'd read in a book the night before. That's what the kids in the book did when they met an alien in another dimension. It means you stare so hard your eyes practically pop out of your head.

Soon half the class was oooing and ahhing. Carefully I pulled the locket over my head and took it off so Sam could get a really good look.

"Gym!" shouted Mrs. Lester.

I figured I'd better not wear the locket to gym so I put it neatly away in the corner of my desk.

We had a really busy day and I guess I kinda forgot about putting my locket back on.

Anyway, just before the last bell, I remembered. Good thing too. Imagine what my mother would say if I went home without it! I opened my desk and reached for it.

It was gone. Gone! I threw everything out of my desk but the locket was nowhere to be found! I felt like I was in an elevator, going down very fast. I couldn't believe what had happened.

The bell rang. I looked around to tell Sam, but she'd already left. I threw everything back into the desk. I felt sick. For a minute I just stood there not knowing what to do. I knew I couldn't stay in the classroom any longer — Mom would ask me why I was late. So I put on my jacket and started out to the car. I prayed she wouldn't notice 'cause if she did I was dead!

Chapter 2

It's Lost!

"It's not fair," I protested. We were in a grocery store. Mom had picked us up from school and taken us there to buy groceries for supper. I was in a terrible mood after what had happened with the locket, and now Ben was making it even worse. It was the last straw.

"Why isn't it fair?" my mother asked. "You have a handful of candy, Ben has a handful of candy."

"But his cost twenty-five cents and mine cost ten cents," I objected, my voice getting higher and louder. I pointed to the prices written on the candy machines.

My mother sighed. She gave me another dime. I put it in the machine and got another handful of SweetTarts.

"You still owe me a nickel," I said. "It's still not fair."

She gave me a look. "All right," she said, "perhaps we should talk about the fifty cents you get every Thursday when you go swimming."

I hate it when she says smart things like that.

Ben looked at my two handfuls of SweetTarts and his one handful of jelly beans. He started to grumble.

"That's not fair. Roz got more than me."

My mother opened the door of the store and started out to the parking lot.

"Coming?" she said, and she looked like she'd just as soon leave us both there.

We followed her out. She grabbed Ben's hand.

As we settled into the car, I prayed she wouldn't ask me the question she's asked me every day since I started kindergarten.

"How was school today, Roz?" she asked, once we were buckled up and driving home. Well, I mean, why should she pick this one day not to ask it? That would be improbable. Meaning, according to my mother, very unlikely.

I didn't reply, of course. How could I tell her that the locket, the very same locket I swore to her I was old enough to take good care of, had disappeared from my desk?

My mother repeated the question. "How was school, Roz?"

Why can't anyone call me by my whole name?

At this point Ben hit me. Of course I hit him back. He started to cry.

"Woz hit me. Woz hit me."

"Rosaline, you're the big one, you know better than to hit him. He'll never learn to stop hitting if you keep doing that."

"But he started it!" I yelled.

"Benjamin," she said, "don't hit."

He wouldn't stop crying, the jerk. He just about kills me, then he cries, and I get yelled at.

Life before Ben, I thought. I'll bet it was great.

If only I could remember more about the four years before he was born. They were probably the best four years of my life.

This year, Mom announced Ben would be going to nursery school at Brock. *My* school. At least I'd always been able to escape him when I went to school. I mean, all the nursery schools in Winnipeg to choose from, and she chooses the one at Brock!

It's a nightmare. His classroom is just down the hall from mine, and as soon as school started in the fall, he got this weird idea that he could come and see me any time. The teachers told him he couldn't. But I don't think he believed them. I think he thought they were teasing him.

So I'll be sitting at my desk working, and then suddenly Ben will be at the door, calling for me. I mean, doesn't his teacher watch those kids? He seems to come and go from that classroom whenever he feels like it.

It's so embarrassing! I thought I'd die the first time he did it. All the kids in the class laughed and said how cute he was.

He's got curly blond hair and blue eyes. I have straight black hair and brown eyes. Everyone thinks he's adorable. But they don't have to live with him. They don't have to come second to him in everything at home.

After we got home from the grocery store that day, the day I lost the locket, I ran straight up to my room and changed into a T-shirt. I was hoping Mom would think I took off the locket when I took off my sweater. The whole time we were in the store, I'd managed to keep my jacket done up.

Mom looked at me when I came downstairs. "You were so cold you kept your jacket done up in the store and now you want to go outside like that? It's not summer yet. Put on your jacket."

She hadn't noticed! I sighed with relief.

I went out to ride my bike before supper. It occurred to me that maybe I should keep riding forever, and never go back home. It would be easier than telling my mom about the locket. What was I going to do?

Chapter 3

Karate Class

At supper time I only ate one hamburger, three potatoes, some corn and a bowl of salad. So my mom got that worried look I really hate.

"Roz, is anything the matter?" she said as she passed the potatoes to Dad.

"No," I answered, maybe a bit too loudly. "Why?"

"Because you've hardly eaten."

She was serious, too. All the kids at school tease me about the lunches I bring every day.

"Hey, Roz," Curtis the Horrible yelled once, "why don't you just rent a truck to carry that lunch bag of yours to school?"

I can never think of anything smart to answer back to Curtis when he says dumb stuff like that. At least, not until I get home. Then I think of lots of answers. Like, "Well, Curtis, you certainly wouldn't need a truck to carry your brain, it's sooo small." Stuff like that.

Of course, Curtis isn't really stupid, just mean. And I wouldn't have dared say anything to his face because he'd have beaten me up — even though I was as tall as he was. I still am. We're the two biggest kids in the class. I've always wondered why he doesn't eat as much as I do.

Anyway, I can't help it if I'm always hungry. Once I tried not to eat as much, but I almost died of starvation. And I'm not fat — not at all — I'm practically skinny. Mom says I'm just growing fast and I'll slow down in a few years and then I won't be so hungry all the time.

"Nothing is wrong," I repeated to Mom with feeling, hoping she would believe me. "Can I be excused?"

"Yes," she said. "Get your jacket, we'd better get going."

"Yeah," piped up Dad, "off you go, I'll clean up."

"Go?" I said. "Where?"

"Roz," my mother sighed, "it's Monday night."

Monday night. Monday night. Oh, no — karate. I'd completely forgotten.

"Oooh, do I have to?"

"Yes," said Mom and she started to glare at me and I could feel Dad's glare too. "Now don't start up again."

I had begged them to enrol me in karate this year, so they did. Then I found out that I was the biggest klutz in the world. I wanted to quit but they wouldn't let me.

"You can quit after this year," Dad had said. "But in this family when we start something, we finish it."

So I was forced to go till the end of the year. And it was a two-hour class. My mom took it with me and she just loved it. She was always practising — surprising us from behind doors and shouting and stuff.

I dragged myself out to the car and off we went.

When we got there, the teacher said we were going to learn throws. First we had to do all our exercises. Then we started on the throws. He needed a volunteer.

I tried to hide behind my mother. Mr. Sun loves to use me as a volunteer, I don't know why.

"Rosaline," he said, and my heart sank, "come up to the mat please."

I stepped out from behind Mom — how had he seen me, did he have X-ray eyes? — and walked as slowly as possible to the mat in the middle of the room.

"Rosaline, just try to punch me," he ordered.

I racked my brain for a good excuse to get out of this. Like, "I'm sorry, Mr. Sun, but I'm going to faint." Or, "I'm sorry, Mr. Sun, but I'm going to throw up," or "I'm sorry, Mr. Sun, but I'm against violence of any sort." I didn't say

thing though. Instead I took a deep breath, made a fist and tried to hit him in the face.

Wham!

Suddenly I was on my back on the mat. He had grabbed my wrist and flipped me over.

Well, that was lots of fun. I staggered to my feet.

"Now you try." He smiled.

He went to hit me. I grabbed his wrist, turned around and pulled. Nothing. I pulled again. Nothing.

"Now I will show everyone step by step." So slowly, step by step, he showed everyone how to flip. Finally he let me go back to Mom, and she and I practised. She flipped me ten times. I almost flipped her once. Sort of. I mean I was pretty close.

"Don't worry, Roz," she said, "you'll get it next time. You almost have it. You just need more confidence."

She always says that to me. But where do you get confidence? Can't just buy it in a store, can you?

I was hungry when we got home. I ate a cold hamburger, an apple, an orange, and a banana. Then my mom made me go to bed. I don't know why. I'm never tired at night but she makes me go to bed anyway. I think I should wait until I'm really tired, but she and Dad are always fussing at me about getting lots of sleep.

As I lay in bed the whole business with the locket came back to me. I guess one good thing about karate was that it made me forget all about the locket.

The locket.

Oh boy, how would I ever sleep when all I could think about was that?

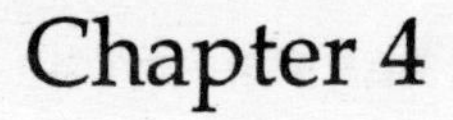

Chapter 4

We're Detectives!

"I have to talk to you," I whispered to Sam as I slipped into my seat the next morning. We were supposed to be getting ready for French.

"I can't talk to you, or play with you," said Sam. "You didn't bring your lion puppet and I told you to."

I hate it when Sam does that. Everything always has to be her way. She loves to boss me around.

I narrowed my eyes and took a good long look around the room. Somewhere in this room, I thought, lurks a crook. Lurks. That's a great word, isn't it? I read it in this mystery book and used my dictionary to find out what it meant. I have a dictionary this year. Everyone in grade three does. But I didn't understand what the dictionary said so I asked my mom. She said it was sort of like being somewhere, but hidden, and you knew someone was up to no good if they were lurking.

Somewhere in this room lurked a crook.

"You have to help me," I whispered to Sam, who usually sits beside me. "Someone stole my locket."

"Really?" said Sam.

"No," I answered, "I'm just kidding."

"Well, you shouldn't kid about stuff like that," she said.

"I'm not kidding," I replied.

"But you said you were," she answered.

"But I was kidding when I said that," I said.

"What?" she said.

"I was kidding when I said I was kidding," I explained.

"You were kidding when you said you were kidding, but you really aren't kidding?" asked Sam.

"Are you kidding?" I asked. "I can't follow you."

"No, I'm not kidding," she said. "You are."

Boy, I could hardly remember what I asked her in the first place.

Oh yeah, my locket, that's what I was asking her about.

"I've lost every necklace I've ever worn but I promised I was old enough not to lose this one! Maybe it was stolen. I know I left it in my desk yesterday and when I went to get it at three-thirty, it was gone."

"Do you think one of the kids took it?" asked Sam.

"What do you think?" I asked back.

"Is everyone ready for French?" called Mrs. Lester. "Come along now, children. Roz, Sam, you don't even have your books out."

"Maybe I should tell Mrs. Lester," I whispered to Sam.

"Yeah," Sam whispered back, "you should. But she's going to tell your mom."

We got into line.

"I'll have to tell Mom, anyway," I went on in a low voice. "But maybe I can wait a day. Maybe we can get it back. Wanna be a detective?"

"Me?" said Sam. Sam is scared of everything. She still sleeps with her light on. It's funny someone so bossy should be such a scaredycat.

"We won't have to go into any dark places, by ourselves, at night, will we?"

"No." I answered. "It must be someone from here who took it. We just have to keep our eyes and ears open. *Wide.*"

"Okay," said Sam. "We'll be detectives. What'll our names be?"

"Umm." I thought for a moment. "Let's see." And I searched my brain for some good names from all those books I'd read. "How about Dynamic Detectives, Dahlia and Dove?"

"Dove," said Sam. "Dove is dumb. Dahlia is nice. I'll be Dahlia."

"No," I objected, "I want to be Dahlia."

"Then I won't play," said Sam.

Once we got to French class we had to stop talking. I like our French teacher. He always makes us laugh.

"I'll be Rose. My own name, sort of," I whispered. "Then we're both flowers."

"Okay," she agreed.

"Now all we have to figure out is where to start."

Chapter 5

Making Plans

It was early in May and the snow had just finished melting. The schoolyard was full of big puddles. Since March, Mom had been complaining about the weather.

Normally, I wouldn't have cared. I love winter because I go skating all the time. But since April it had been getting warm, then cold, then warm again, so the ice on the rinks was all melted and yucky. It was boring not being able to skate. Then finally we were able to put away our boots and get into sneakers and jackets, and I could ride my bike. But Mom still made me keep my hood up when I left the house for school. I never put it up at recess, though. I didn't want everyone laughing at me.

So it was recess and it was pretty windy and I was thinking that maybe I should put my hood up even though I'd look silly. Sam had hers up. She didn't care what the other kids said.

"Are we detectives now?" she asked.

"Of course, Dahlia," I answered.

"So what do we do, Rose?" she continued.

"Well," I answered, not quite sure myself, "I guess we have to spy on everyone. We have to follow everyone around and see if they're wearing the locket."

It was sort of exciting. Just like in my mystery books.

"Okay," she said.

I put my hands behind my back and began to stroll around the school yard. Curtis and Brian had found the biggest puddle in the yard. They were jumping in it. What a mess. Their feet and pants were soaking wet. Mrs. Lester was going to be mad. She was going to say, "This is not a

kindergarten class, we do not keep extra clothes for those who get wet in water play." But then she'd go find them extra socks from the Lost and Found so they wouldn't catch cold. She's too nice to them. They deserve to have wet feet all day if they jump in puddles. But she can't help it. That's just the way she is.

Sam and I circled the school yard, staring at everyone in our class. But they all had jackets on and we couldn't see anything. Maybe this wasn't such a great plan. It certainly wasn't working out the way it did in my books.

"You know," Sam said, coming up to me, "this wasn't such a great plan. I'll think of the next one." She loves to be the boss.

"Okay," I said, "you think of a better one."

"I will!" she said.

"Well?" I pressed.

"I'm thinking," she replied.

"Well?" I said again.

"I'm still thinking," she answered.

The bell rang.

"I'll have a plan by lunch time," Sam declared.

"Okay, lunch," I said.

I can walk home from school at noon, but I like to stay for lunch. Sam stays and we play together. At home I'd be really bored and I'd have to see Ben. He trails around after me and won't leave me alone and drives me crazy.

I didn't care what Sam said — I hadn't given up on my plan. I looked closely at everyone in our class. No luck. At lunch I looked closely at everyone again. No luck.

I guess the person who stole the locket wouldn't be stupid enough to wear it, I thought to myself. They'd be more likely to hide it. Of course. We'd have to look around the classroom. Maybe it was hidden there.

Sam was sitting next to me, eating a peanut butter and jam sandwich (yuck). I was eating corned beef on rye with a dill pickle and mustard, and juice, and two cookies, and some taco chips, and strawberries, and a banana.

Sam said, her mouth all sticky so she could hardly talk (double yuck), "I have a plan. We have to look in the classroom."

"I just thought the same thing," I said, speaking as fast as I could. I can't afford to do too much talking at lunch. I have a lot of food to eat. I concentrate very hard on getting finished.

"Great minds think alike," she said. "But I don't want to do it."

"Yeah," I said, my mouth full of chips, "it's dangerous. What if Mrs. Lester catches us? She could think we're the crooks."

"Yeah," said Sam, "let's forget it."

"No," I said, gobbling up my fruit and Sam's apple core (what a waste, I always tell her), "we have to try. Come on. We'll look around when we go get our jackets after lunch. After all, maybe the locket just dropped out of my desk and someone picked it up, or it's still on the floor or something."

"Well, okay," Sam agreed. "If it's just to look around a bit."

I slowed down with my eating so the other kids would get outside before we did. Then we went to the classroom for our jackets. No one was around.

You don't realize how much junk everyone keeps in a classroom until you start looking for something. We found wads of bubble gum stuck in a corner, half-eaten erasers, pencils, empty Twizzler packages and Skittle wrappers on the floor, books and notebooks everywhere — but no locket.

"Should we look in everyone's desk and tote tray?" I whispered to Sam. Our desks can't hold all our stuff, so we each have a basket, called a tote tray, for our extra things.

"No!" she exclaimed.

"Well, I don't want to, either," I said, "but we are detectives and we should leave no stone unturned."

"What does that mean?" Sam asked.

"It means we should try everything," I answered. "Except maybe looking in people's desks and tote trays. We'd better think about that some more."

"Yeah," Sam said, "let's think outside."

Just then Ben and my mother appeared at the door.

"I have an appointment downtown, Roz. Will you watch Ben until the bell rings?"

I nodded, my heart pounding in my chest. Suddenly I knew why detectives' hearts always pound in their chests.

Mother stood still and looked at me.

"Why aren't you girls outside with everyone else? Won't you get in trouble for being here?"

Ben grabbed me by my jacket.

"I wanna go on the climber." He dragged me out of the classroom past my mom.

I let him. I sort of shrugged and smiled at Mom. She gave us a strange look, as if she was thinking, I wonder what they've been up to.

Thank goodness for Ben, I thought. Then I couldn't believe I'd thought it. I was probably loosing my marbles due to all the stress.

Anyway, we had to think of another plan.

Fast.

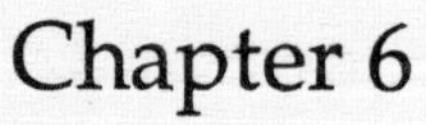

Chapter 6

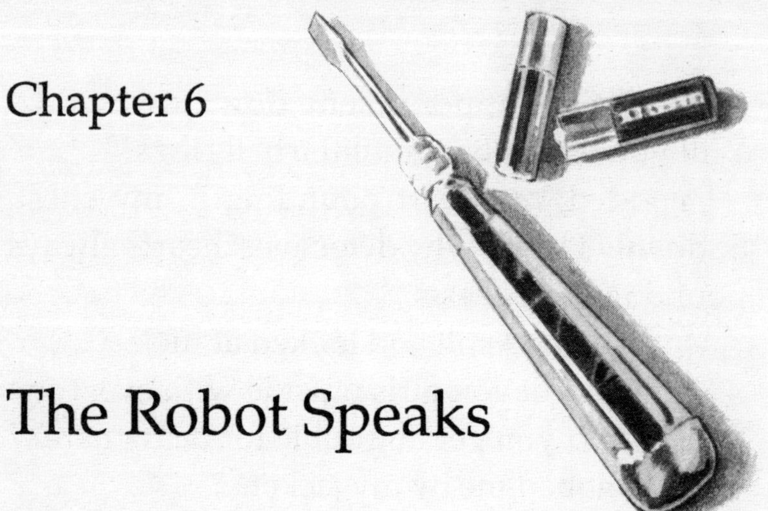

The Robot Speaks

After school that day I went to Hebrew School. I sort of like it. I'm learning Hebrew and about what the Jewish people did in the olden days. I always walk with David who's also in my class at regular school. We go twice a week. David is okay but he only wants to play robots and stuff. Which is also okay but not *all the time.*

"Hey," I said to him, "want to be a spy?" I was thinking that maybe he'd seen something or maybe he would help Sam and me look for the locket.

"Sure," David replied. "My name is Mechanis

Mechanico and I'm a robot spy from the planet Spyaticus." And he started walking like a robot.

"Okay," I sighed. (No use trying to get him to be a person.) "I'm Rose and I'm on the lookout for a super-valuable gold magical locket that has great power. Anyone owning such a locket would have enough power to rule the universe!"

"I will rule the universe," said David in a monotone. "I will own the gold locket. Where is it?"

"I don't know!" I exclaimed. "That's what we have to find out!"

"Simple," said David. "We use our X-ray vision to see through the universe until we find it."

"I don't think we have to search the entire universe," I said. "I think maybe, uh, our classroom at Brock should be good enough."

"I have already seen such a thing in the classroom at Brock school," David announced.

"You've what?" I exclaimed. "You've seen it? Where?"

"I do not remember," he continued in his monotone. "My memory banks must need re-charging. Must need recharging. Must need re-charging."

"Yeah, but think!" I said.

"I can't think, my batteries are running out, out, out." Then he stopped as if frozen and pretended he couldn't move.

I opened a pretend panel on his back and put some pretend batteries into it.

"Good as new," I said. "I've put in fresh bat-teries."

"Thank you," he said, once again moving like a robot. "I will not forget this."

"No, really, David," I urged, "did you really see a gold locket? Because I really lost one yes-terday. Remember, the one I was showing eve-ryone yesterday morning?"

"Yes," said David, still being a robot, "I saw it. But where? Where did I see it? Please check my memory circuits. Are they working?"

I pretended to open him up again, this time his head, and take a look.

"No, they're all scrambled up," I said.

"Fix them," he said. "Maybe then I will remember."

I pretended to fool around with tools on the back of his head.

"There," I said, trying not to get annoyed, "all fixed. Now do you remember?"

"No," he said. "That is to say, yes."

"Which?" I said. "No or yes?"

"Both," he said.

"Both no and yes?" I asked.

"Yes," he said.

"Yes, you remember?" I questioned.

"No," he said.

"No, you forget?" I said.

"Yes," he said.

"Yes what?" I screamed in frustration.

"Yes, no, I forget where, but yes, I remember it."

Oh boy, isn't that right where we started?

"But you must remember," I said, ready to bop him. "Try harder."

"I am trying too hard," he protested. "My

circuits are beginning to overheat. I am going to blow up. KABOOM." He pretended to explode and threw himself all over the place.

"Did you lose a locket, really?" he said, as he dusted himself off.

"Yes," I replied, "really, and my mom is going to kill me. It was from my great-grandmother."

"That's too bad," David said. "I really did see a beautiful gold locket yesterday. I wish I could remember . . . someone had it in the lunch room . . . oh yeah, I think it was Curtis."

"Curtis!" I exclaimed. "Oh no, not Curtis!" Why did it have to be the meanest kid in class?

But how did he get it? Did he steal it, or just find it on the floor? And what was I going to do about it? Could I just go up to him and ask him if he had found it? Maybe, if I did that, he'd give it right back. Or maybe he'd pretend he didn't know what I was talking about, and he'd hide it and I'd never see it again. I sighed. I was in a real mess.

"You don't look too good," said David to me as we walked up the steps to Hebrew school.

"I don't feel so good," I answered. "Will you keep an eye out for me?" I asked. "If you see Curtis with the locket will you tell me?"

"Sure," David agreed. "You should tell Mrs. Lester," he suggested. "She could ask Curtis for it back."

We walked into our classroom and sat down at our desks. I imagined going right up to Curtis and demanding the locket back. Then I imagined what it would feel like to get hit by Curtis. I imagined my mother asking me where the locket was, maybe asking me to wear it. Trouble is, I could imagine everything except what to say to her.

It was a mess all right. A real mess. A real conundrum. What a great word that is. It means problem. And I certainly had a big one. A great big conundrum.

Chapter 7

What Do You Do With a Bully?

I'm the oldest, right? But do I get to go to sleep latest? Oh no. In fact Ben goes to bed at the same time I do and he's four years younger than me. Four. Now is that fair?

And I can't have sweets after supper because too much sugar makes *Ben* wild. Is that fair? And try to get two words out at supper time. Ben starts to sing at the top of his lungs and I start to shout at him and Mom starts to shout at both of us and Dad tries to pretend he's in Hawaii and it ends up I never do finish saying what I started to say. Is that fair?

That same day, that is, the night of that same day, I tried to ask Mom and Dad a question at supper time.

"What would you do," I said, "if this big bully —" Ben started to sing, "— if this big bully," I continued, screaming as loud as I could, "had something that was yours? SHUT UP, BEN!"

Ben kept right on singing.

"Ben," said my mother, "Roz is trying to talk. Please be quiet and wait your turn. You can sing to us when she's finished."

But Ben continued to sing — if that's what you can call it. Really, he just repeats the same thing over and over again at the top of his lungs. That night he was singing Bully.

"But this is a bully song," he objected, putting that hurt look on.

"I know, honey," said Mom, "and it's a lovely song but we'll hear it after Roz finishes. What was the question again, Roz?"

I sighed. "If a bully —"

Ben started again.

"Bully, bully, bully, bully." There was no tune, of course.

"Ben," said my mother, "if you can't be quiet you'll have to leave the table and go up to your room. Wait until Roz is finished, then we'll listen."

Of course he wouldn't wait. He just kept yelling, "Bully, bully."

Mom got up to pick him out of his chair. Finally he stopped.

"Thank you," said Mom. "Now, Roz, what was it?"

"If a bully had something that was yours, what would you do?"

"Well," said Mom, "I would go up to him and ask him for it."

"What if he says he doesn't have it but you know he does?"

"I would say I know he has it and I want it back," Mom answered.

"What if he hits you?" I went on.

"Roz," said Dad, "you know we don't believe in violence as a solution to any problem. It's always better to talk. But if someone hit me, I'd hit him back. Then he'd think twice before he hit me again."

"But I can't hit him," I objected. "He'll kill me!"

The truth is I was scared stiff of Curtis. I hated the rough games he played at recess and I hated the thought of getting hurt.

"How about a karate flip?" suggested Mom.

"Oh, sure." I laughed. "Fat chance."

"What about your karate defense moves? I'll bet you could stop a punch now," said Mom.

"Nah," I grunted.

"Well," she stated, "I believe in the direct approach. Ask him. Who knows, maybe he'll be very nice about it. Maybe he doesn't even know this thing is yours. By the way," she continued, "what is it of yours that this bully has?"

"BULLY, BULLY, BULLY." Ben started up again.

Mom sighed.

"All right, Ben, your turn."

We all had to listen to him scream for the rest

of supper. But I was very relieved. At least I didn't have to answer Mom's question. What would I have said? "Oh it's nothing, Mom, just great-grandmother's locket that you told me not to lose."

That night, before I fell asleep, I lay in bed listening to my rock tapes on the little cassette player I got for Chanukkah and tried to figure out a plan.

Should I just walk up to Curtis and demand the locket back? No, he'd pretend he didn't have it.

Should I tell Mrs. Lester? No, then for sure he'd pretend not to have it.

I'd have to catch him with it. I just hoped he hadn't sold it or anything. That was something I wouldn't put past him. I'd have to get Sam and David to help me. One of us would have to watch Curtis at all times. And one of us would have to check his tote tray. I just didn't want that to be me. He'd kill me if he caught me.

Karate or not, I didn't want to get into a fight with Curtis. I'm too young to die, I thought.

Way too young.

Just then my mother stuck her head in the door.

"Roz, Baba has invited us to dinner at her house Friday night," she said. "Be sure to wear your locket. She'll be so happy to see that I've passed it on to you!"

"Sure, Mom," I croaked, barely able to get the words out.

" 'Night, dear."

" 'Night."

Well, disaster had struck! I'd have to get the locket off Curtis or face my mother and my grandmother! What a choice!

Chapter 8

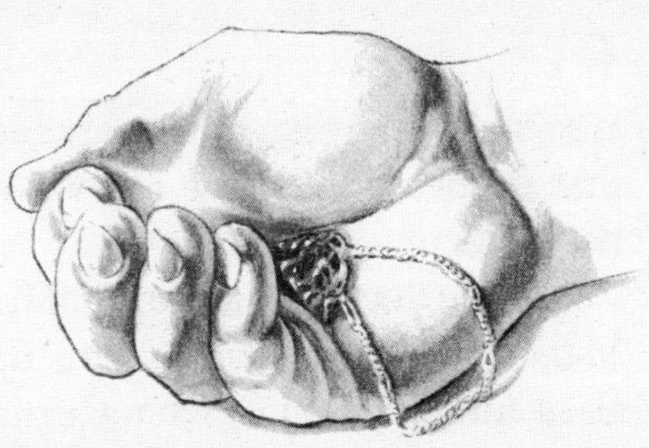

A Rotten Recess

The first thing we did at school the next morning was math. I used to hate math but Mrs. Lester makes it fun and this year I've been getting all VG's.

A small group of us sat around a table with Mrs. Lester while the other kids worked at their desks. And guess who ended up sitting right beside me? Curtis. Now, you'd think Curtis, being the jerk he is, would also be a stupid jerk. But the weird thing is, he's smart. Especially in math.

Anyway, what I can't understand is, if Curtis

is so smart, why isn't he smart enough to know that bullies don't have friends and everyone hates them?

Well, he does have a couple of friends, I guess: Mark and Rudy. They're the stupidest kids in class and they do just what Curtis tells them to do. That's not what I call being friends. Of course, I do what Sam wants me to do, but that's different. After all, we're best friends.

I glanced over at Curtis. He sure looked big. He's much heavier than I am. He has a big head and lots of brown hair which falls all over. He wasn't wearing the locket. But then, why would he? A boy wouldn't wear a girl's locket.

So why did he steal it if he didn't want to wear it? Maybe he did just find it. What if, I thought, I just ask him how he got it? That couldn't hurt, could it? I'd do it at recess. For sure.

"Roz," Mrs. Lester asked, "are you with us today? You seem to be in a world of your own."

I giggled. I giggle a lot. I can't help it.

"I'm here, Mrs. Lester," I said. Curtis snickered.

The morning seemed to drag on and on and on. Finally the recess bell rang, and I told Sam my plan on the way out to the playground. "I'll just go right up to him and ask him," I declared. "And you'll come with me."

"Do I have to?" she said.

"You want me to go alone?" I asked.

"I don't want you to go alone," said Sam. "But I don't want you to take me with you, either."

"Aren't you my friend?" I demanded.

"You wouldn't ask a friend to get into trouble, would you?" she replied.

That was a hard one to answer. Sometimes Sam is just too smart.

"No," I said at last. "I wouldn't ask a friend, a friend wouldn't need to be asked. A friend would just want to do it."

Sam sighed. She couldn't think of a good excuse for that one.

We started over to where Curtis, Mark and Rudy were playing superheroes. Curtis was screaming an order, his arms in the air, his voice loud. In his hand he held a shiny gold object.

"With the power invested in me by this treasure I command you to bow before me," he yelled.

The boys bowed.

"Now, go slay the dragon of DunLevy, and bring me back his wings."

Mark and Rudy drew their swords and charged off down the playground to get the dragon.

Actually it looked like a really neat game. I wouldn't have minded playing.

"Roz," said Sam, "look at what he's holding in his hand!"

I moved in closer. The treasure was none other than my locket. My locket! I ran up to Curtis, forgetting to be afraid.

"Curtis, Curtis, that's my locket! Give it here!"

Curtis lowered his arm and looked at the locket. Then he looked at me.

"Prove it," he said.

I was flabbergasted. (A word used a lot in spooky novels — people are always flabbergasted when they see a ghost or

something — it means they can't believe their eyes, or in this case, their ears.)

For a moment I didn't speak. He was standing there with his hands on his hips, looking like he'd love a fight.

"It's my locket," I repeated, "and I want it back. If you need proof, open it up. There are pictures of my great-grandparents inside."

Instead of opening it up, he slipped it into his jacket pocket.

"Finders keepers."

"You give that back, Curtis," I said, "or I'll tell Mrs. Lester."

"If you do," he said, "I'll tell her I had it, but I lost it."

"You wouldn't!" I exclaimed.

"I would," he declared. "And you couldn't prove it's not true."

"Yes I could, we'll have you searched!" I shouted.

"Then I'll throw it away somewhere you'll never find it!" he shouted back.

"You're rotten, Curtis!" I screamed. "You

won't get away with this!"

"Oh yes, I will," he laughed. "Maybe I'll give it back to you when I'm finished playing with it — if you're lucky."

"Why I'll . . . I'll . . . " I felt like I could kill him. But I was also afraid I was going to burst out crying.

Just then the bell rang.

"You'll what?" He snickered again and pushed me as he ran past me towards the classroom.

I stood there, in the middle of the playground, not knowing what to do. And feeling awful. Could he get away with it?

At that moment everything in life seemed pretty unfair. And the prospect of having to tell my mom the whole story was getting too close for comfort. What a disaster!

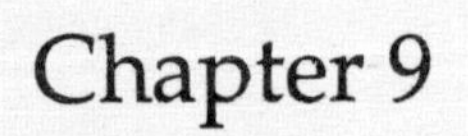

Chapter 9

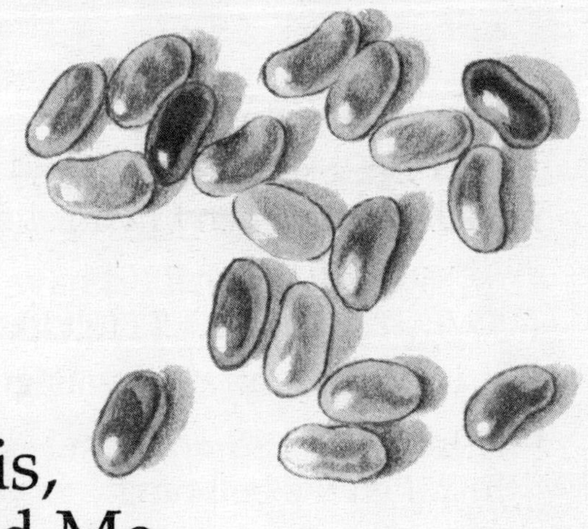

Ben, Curtis, Karate and Me

"Come on," said Sam, "we'll be late. Don't just stand there."

"I can't believe anyone could be so rotten," I said, stamping my foot in anger. "Can you?"

"Yes," said Sam, "if it's Curtis. Come on."

She grabbed my arm and pulled me along.

Mrs. Lester was talking as we walked into the classroom.

"Hurry and take off your jackets, girls," she said. "We'll be working on our science projects this afternoon."

Sam and I went to the back of the class where there are open closets. I put my jacket on a hook. Then I noticed that Curtis's jacket was hanging a few hooks over. All I'd have to do was reach my hand in and grab my locket.

I looked around. Curtis was staring at me. So what? I could still do it, and he'd be too late to stop me.

"Hurry up, girls, right now," Mrs Lester said.

Rats. She was staring right at me. I'd have to wait till later.

Sam and I hurried over to the supply corner and got all our junk. We were making a model of the solar system out of papier mâché. We coloured the planets, and put rings around the ones that needed rings, and connected everything with wire. I was glad we were doing the project together because it gave us a chance to talk.

David came over and sat down with us for a minute.

"I saw all that," he remarked. "Bad."

"Yeah," I agreed, "but what can I do about it?"

"There has to be something," he said, "just think."

He gave me an encouraging smile, then left to work on his own project.

"He's right," I said to Sam, "we have to think."

"You should tell Mrs. Lester," said Sam.

"And then Curtis would throw the locket away so I'll never find it," I answered.

"How could he do that here, in the class?" Sam asked.

"Good point," I replied. "Maybe he couldn't. Maybe I should tell Mrs. Lester. But what if Curtis throws the locket out the window or something? He'd be in trouble anyway. A little more trouble wouldn't matter. And he'd want to get back at me for telling. So he probably would throw it out the window and it'd land in a very deep mud puddle and I'd never find it again. Or it would break, and how would I explain *that* to my mom?"

I stopped to think.

"There must be a way," I said, "there must be."

Suddenly it dawned on me.

"It's simple. I just have to walk over to the jackets when no one is looking, stick my hand in his jacket pocket and take the locket out."

"He'll see you. You'll never get away with it," Sam said. "He'll run over and grab his jacket."

"We need a diversion," I said.

"A what?" asked Sam.

"A diversion. A big commotion that attracts everyone's attention so they aren't looking at you."

Just then Ben came bursting into the room.

"Oh no," I groaned. "Not again."

"Yeah," sighed Sam, "now there's a commotion."

"Sam!" I exclaimed, "of course!"

Ben was running around the room looking for me, calling, "Woz, Woz."

Mrs. Lester just ignored him. She always expects me to take him back to his room.

But this time I decided I wouldn't take him right back to his room. No, this time I had a better idea.

"Ben, we're over here," I called.

He saw me and ran over.

"Ben," I said, "you have to stay in your nursery class. Mrs. Browning is going to worry about you."

"I wanted to see you," he said. "I was lonely."

Mom says he loves me more than anyone in the world. But does he have to be such a pest about it?

"Ben," I said, "want to know a secret?"

"Yes," he said, his eyes shining.

"Do you know who Curtis is?" I asked him.

"No," he answered, shaking his head, his big blue eyes looking up into mine.

"He's that kid over there," I whispered, "wearing the army shirt and pants."

"G.I. Joe?" asked Ben.

"Yeah," I replied. "And G.I. Joe has jelly beans in all his pockets and he told me if you came to class you could climb on him and tickle him and try to get the candies."

"Really?" said Ben, his eyes opening very wide.

For a minute I thought that maybe I was being rotten, but I quickly shook off that thought. After all, I needed my locket back, no matter what.

"Yes, really," I said. "Go on, get them now."

Curtis was sitting on the floor at the far end of the room. Ben ran over and jumped on him yelling, "Candy, candy."

I headed for the jackets. I heard Curtis yelling, "Get off me. Get off me, you stupid baby."

I found Curtis's jacket, and I put my hand in one pocket. It was filled with junk. How was I going to find the locket in that mess?

"Ben, Ben," Mrs. Lester, called, "come down off Curtis, Ben. Someone is going to get hurt. Roz, where are you?"

I put my other hand in Curtis's other pocket. I could feel old jelly beans, nails, candy wrappers, but I couldn't feel my locket.

"Rosaline! What are you doing?" Mrs. Lester was looking straight at me. "Please help us with your brother."

Curtis was struggling to his feet. I ran over to

him just in time to see him shake Ben to the floor. Ben landed with a crash and started to cry. Mrs. Lester put her arms around him.

"Curtis, that was not necessary," she said in a very mad voice.

I ran over to Ben.

"Are you alright?" I asked him, kneeling on the floor.

He was bawling his head off.

"You, you, you told me," he said, his big blue eyes accusing me. Then he started to cry so hard he couldn't talk. He must have bumped himself when he fell.

"There, there," Mrs. Lester said, "you'll soon be fine, Ben. Now let's go back to Mrs. Browning and we'll check to see if there are any bruises or cuts." She took his hand and led him out of the room.

I went back to the corner Sam was sitting in.

Sam looked at me.

"Well?" she asked.

I shook my head.

"Nothing," I said.

I sat down. I felt pretty bad. No locket, and well, I felt sorry I'd done that to Ben. He did what I told him because he trusted me.

I guess he does love me, I thought. But I don't give him much love back.

And then I looked up to see Curtis coming toward me, his face all mad.

"Hey," he yelled, "you keep your dumb brother off me."

I started to get up. Sam put a hand on my arm. "Don't, Roz," she warned.

I shook her hand off and got up.

"Don't call my brother dumb," I said.

"Okay," said Curtis. "He's not dumb, he's an idiot. And a dolt. And a nerd. That better?"

"Just like you?" I answered back.

"Why, you . . . " yelled Curtis and went to punch me.

Well, I guess that karate class did teach me something because suddenly it was like everything was happening in slow motion. I saw his fist coming toward my face. I moved my arm up and I blocked the punch, grabbed his arm,

turned, and heaved with all my might — and flipped him onto his back!

The whole class cheered, even Mark and Rudy.

Just then Mrs. Lester walked back in.

"What is going on here?" she exclaimed.

Curtis scrambled up. It almost looked like he was going to cry.

"Nothing," he muttered, and hurried back to his project.

"Roz?" she asked.

"Nothing, Mrs. Lester," I said.

"Everyone, back to work," she ordered.

I went up to her.

"How is Ben?" I asked.

"He's fine, Roz, but please try to talk to him about staying in his room."

"I will, Mrs. Lester, I promise. Thanks." I went back to Sam and sank down to the floor. I felt sort of shaky. I couldn't believe what had just happened.

Curtis was looking at me nervously from the other end of the room.

"Are you crazy?" said Sam. "He could have killed you."

"Well, he didn't," I answered. "And if I hadn't done something he *would* have killed me."

Then I looked at her.

"And while I think of it — I don't like the way you boss me around all the time. You shouldn't make the rules about what toy I have to bring, that's not fair."

Sam stared at me. Boy, was she surprised.

"Yeah," she said, "I guess you're right. I'll try not to do it any more."

Wow! It was my turn to be surprised. I never figured sticking up for myself would be so easy. I felt a lot better. I'd stood up for Ben and for myself.

But I still didn't have my locket.

Chapter 10

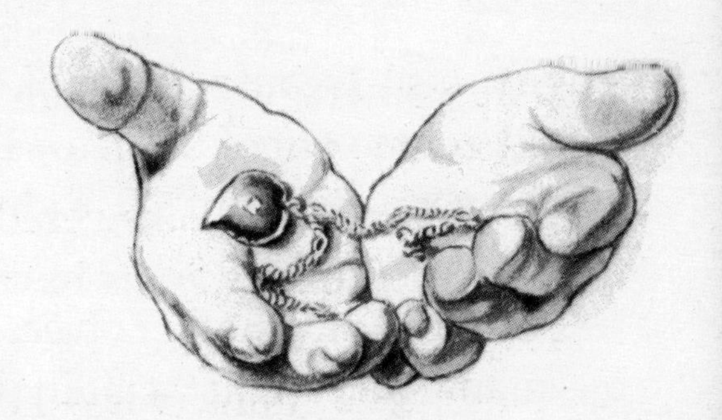

Learning a Lesson

"Roz," Mom said to me at supper time, "what is this story about Ben getting hurt in your classroom today?"

My heart sank.

"Oh that," I said.

"Yes," she said. "That. But what is that? Ben says you told him Curtis had candies for him, and then Curtis hurt him."

I was in a real fix, that's for sure. I didn't know what to do. Just blab the whole story out and get it over with? Or try to stall for just a bit longer until I could think of something that would get me out of this jam? I tried to stall.

"I'm sorry," I said, "I didn't think Curtis would hurt him."

"But, Roz," my mother objected, "you've told me many times what a bully Curtis is. Now, what happened exactly? Exactly," she repeated.

It didn't look like stalling was working.

"Well," I muttered, "I was trying to create a diversion."

"A diversion?" questioned Dad. "Why?"

"Well," I said even more softly, "I wanted to do something without Curtis seeing me do it, and that's why I told Ben to go over to him and tickle him."

"You used Ben," said Mom in a very quiet voice.

I nodded my head.

"Curtis hurted me," Ben declared, looking like he was going to cry again.

"Sorry, Ben," I muttered. "I didn't think, really, about what would happen to you."

"Well, I'm not sure sorry is good enough,"

said Mom. "What do you think?" she asked Dad.

"I'd like to know what was so important she was willing to sacrifice her own brother," said Dad.

Oh boy, things were getting worse and worse.

"Well, I didn't think of it like that," I stalled.

"No," Mom remarked, "you didn't think, did you?"

Oh boy, I was really in trouble. I was definitely in more trouble than if I'd told them I'd lost the locket in the first place. Because then I'd only have been in trouble for losing it, not for losing it and not telling them and getting Ben hurt.

"Well," I said, "remember great-grandmother's locket?" Oh, I felt sick. Positively sick. Maybe I'd faint and I wouldn't have to tell them. They'd be so worried they would forget all about the whole thing.

"Yes?" they replied together.

"Locket, locket, locket," Ben started to sing. "Just a minute!" He got up from the table and ran upstairs.

"Where are you going?" called Dad.

But Ben didn't answer. He never does.

"Well . . ." I started, wondering how I could put this so it wouldn't sound so bad. There didn't seem to be a way. I stopped.

"Yes?" Mom said. "Go on."

"Okay," I said, and I took a deep breath. I felt like someone standing in front of a firing squad. "I took the locket off," I said, talking really fast to get it over with, "and put it in my desk and really it was safe, Mom, but Curtis stole it. Or found it," I added. "I'm not sure which. And then he wouldn't give it back. But I knew he'd put it in his jacket pocket so I told Ben to look for candy on him and I went to check out Curtis's pockets but I couldn't find the locket."

"What do you mean, he wouldn't give it back?" said Dad.

"Just what I said. He wouldn't. He said he'd throw it away if I told Mrs. Lester."

"Don't you think you should have told us?" Mom demanded.

"Yeah," I said, "but he never would have admitted it to a grownup."

"Still," said Dad, "what you did to Ben was wrong."

"It wasn't fair," Mom said.

"No," I agreed, making a face, feeling like I was going to cry, "I guess it wasn't."

Well, this was it. The absolute pits. That means the bottom. Rock bottom. And I'd hit it. My parents knew I'd lied. They were looking at me with that disappointed look that's worse than yelling. I'd hurt Ben, and I still didn't have the locket. My only consolation, the only thing that made me feel better, was the thought that things couldn't get any worse.

"Well, I'll just have to phone Curtis's parents," Mom said, getting up from her chair. "Then he'll have to give the locket back."

Okay. I was wrong. Things could get worse!

"No!" I almost screamed. "No! You can't! Curtis will deny it and then he'll throw the locket away so we can't prove he took it and we'll never find it and then he'll come to school and go after me again. Although," I added, "he doesn't scare me any more!"

"Well then, Roz," Mom said, folding her arms, "if I don't phone his parents what would you suggest? If you can't think of anything else, I will certainly phone."

I mashed my vegetables around with my fork. But I couldn't come up with one idea, even though I was racking my brain. I could feel the tears starting to burn my eyes.

Just then Ben came running into the kitchen. He climbed into his chair. His fist was all clenched up. He put it in my face.

"Don't," I said, getting peeved with him again.

He opened his hand.

A small gold locket lay in his palm.

I stared at it. I couldn't believe my eyes.

"My locket! Ben, where did you get my locket?"

"In Curtis's pocket," said Ben. "You told me

he had candy for me. But he got mad at me and pushed me. He was bad. You should always use words when you're mad."

I reached for the locket.

"Mine," he protested. He closed his fist over it.

"Ben," said Mom, "it is Roz's locket."

"Just a minute," I said.

I ran up to my room and threw things around on my desk until I found a small brown bag. I ran downstairs, and sat down again at the table.

"Trade?" I said to Ben.

"What?" he asked.

I took out a big chocolate egg all wrapped in gold. Sam had given it to me at Easter. I'd been saving it.

Ben's eyes lit up.

"Trade," he said.

He handed me the locket.

I actually felt like kissing him. I never kiss him. But I did. I kissed him.

"YUCK," he yelled, wiping his cheek. "I hate kisses."

About the Author

Carol Matas didn't always want to be a writer — she started out as an actor, and began to write while expecting her first child. Now she is the author of more than two dozen best-selling books for children and young adults, including *Daniel's Story*, *Rebecca*, *Cloning Miranda* and *Footsteps in the Snow*.

Carol's books have won many honours, including the Silver Birch Award and the Red Maple Award. She lives in Winnipeg, Manitoba.